PRISCILLA GORILLA

Barbara Bottner and Michael Emberley

A CAITLYN DLOUHY BOOK

Atheneum Books for Young Readers

New York   London   Toronto   Sydney   New Delhi

When Priscilla turned six,
her dad gave her a book called
ALL ABOUT GORILLAS.
They read it a million skillion times!

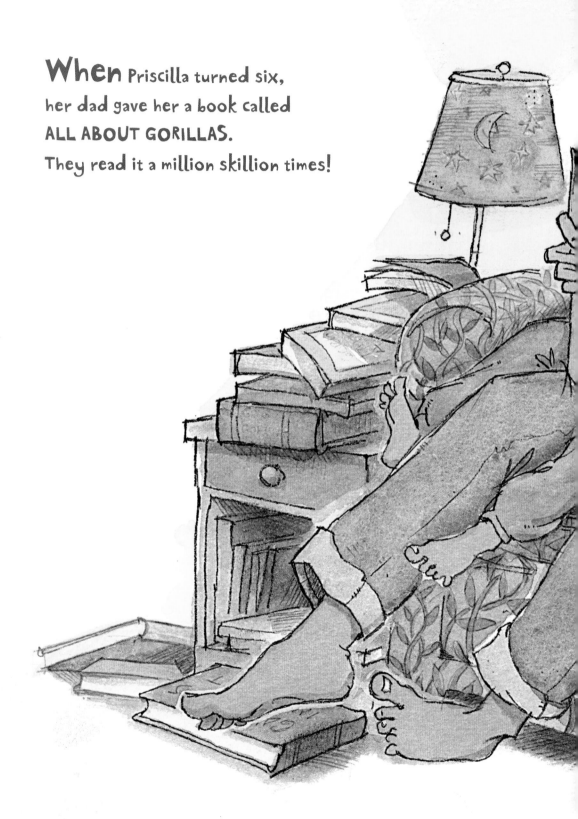

Priscilla talked about gorillas morning, noon, and night.

On Science Day
she drew a picture
of their habitats.

On Famous Person Day she brought
a poster of Dian Fossey.

On Events Day she performed her own original gorilla dance.

Before she went to sleep she wrote in her private GORILLA GAZETTE.

"Why do you love gorillas so much?" her mother asked.

"They always get their way,"
said Priscilla.

"Hmmm," said her mother. "You already get your way a lot."

"Not in Mr. Todd's class.
I was teaching Lily my gorilla dance
during nap time and Mr. Todd
invited me to the Thinking Corner,"
Priscilla explained.

"Did you do any thinking?"

"I was thinking how I don't like the Thinking Corner."

The next afternoon, before the class photo,
everyone was supposed to bring a report about their favorite animal.

The best part was that you could dress up to look like them.

So Priscilla
put her
gorilla pajamas on
over her
school clothes
and kissed
her mother
good-bye.

Priscilla was the last person to give her report:

"Gorillas say hello by rubbing their noses together.

"They can't swim. They laugh and cry.

And they have very long arms."

"Very good, Priscilla," said Mr. Todd.
"You may sit down."

"I'm not done," said Priscilla.
"They can grasp things with
their hands or their feet."

"THANK YOU," said Mr. Todd.

"And they sleep ten hours a day!
The end."

Everyone clapped.

On the way back to her seat,
Priscilla grumbled to her friend Lily,

What I really love about gorillas
is that nobody bothers them.

"Now it's time for the class photo," said Mr. Todd.
"Let's take off our costumes."

"I think I'd rather stay a gorilla,"
Priscilla said.

"Sorry, sweetie,
there can't be any gorillas
in the class photo,"
said Mr. Todd.
"That would ruin the picture
for everyone."

Priscilla polled the class:
"Do you think
it will ruin the photo
if I am a gorilla?"

There were a lot of
noisy opinions.

"**Everyone,**
please line up for your pictures.

"And, Priscilla,
I'm inviting you
to the Thinking Corner again."

Priscilla growled.

Rrrrr...!

"I'm not a troublemaker,"
Priscilla snorted.
"I'm a gorilla!!"
She beat her chest.

"I wasn't in the class picture today,"
Priscilla told her mother that night.

"Why not?"

"Mr. Todd thought I belonged
in the Thinking Corner again.
He's a bad teacher."

"I'm sure there is more to it than that,"
said Priscilla's mother.

The next day,
Lily wore her lion pajamas to class.
She told Mr. Todd,
"I love lions as much as
Priscilla loves gorillas."

Lily's lion roared at Priscilla's gorilla.

Lily was invited to join Priscilla in the Thinking Corner.

You are my VERY best friend,

Priscilla
whispered.

Sam said:
"You're both troublemakers!"

"I was just being a gorilla.
Nobody tells a gorilla
what to wear,"
Priscilla told Sam.

"Gorillas don't wear anything," said Sam.

The next day, the Thinking Corner was crowded.

"I love your pajamas,"
Priscilla told everyone.

"We are running out of room in the Thinking Corner,"
Priscilla told her parents when she came home from school.

Priscilla's father opened up **ALL ABOUT GORILLAS**.
"It says here that gorillas mostly help each other. They've lasted
all these millions of years because they **COOPERATE**.

Is that the **kind** of gorilla you are?"

"I'm more of a troublemaker gorilla,"
Priscilla said.

"Well, if you like being a troublemaker,
maybe you want to be a **different** animal. Like a skunk?"

That night, Priscilla studied her collection of gorillas.

In the morning, she went up to Mr. Todd.
"My ALL ABOUT GORILLAS book
says even gorillas
don't always get their way."

"If that is an apology,
I accept it, Priscilla," said Mr. Todd.

Priscilla returned to her desk in the second row.

"Now, class," said Mr. Todd, "please put on your coats.

We're going on an adventure!

And, Priscilla, it looks like your gorilla pajamas might come in handy."

Everyone climbed on
the school bus
and drove to the zoo.

They headed straight to the Ape House.

Priscilla ran over to the massive window.
The biggest gorilla of all was grooming his sister.

Now he came
to the front of the cage.
His big brown eyes
looked right at Priscilla.

He grunted and licked his lips.

"What do you know about gorillas?"
Mr. Todd asked the class.

"They sleep ten hours a day," said Lily.

"They can't swim," said Zoe.

"They laugh and cry," said Walter and Kirby.

"THEY COOPERATE WITH EACH OTHER!" Priscilla shouted.

Priscilla pounded her chest and hooted. She did her famous gorilla dance. The gorilla bounced up and down, hooting back.

Simian Primate

Uganda Zaire

Eastern Lowland Gorilla (gorilla graueri)

"And they dance!"
cried Sam.

Sam started doing
his own gorilla dance.

So did Lily, then
Miranda, then
Walter and Zoe.

Then,
everyone!

Even Mr. Todd!

To all the little gorillas. Especially Miranda and Brandon
—B. B.

For Rick, thank you
—M. E.

ATHENEUM BOOKS FOR YOUNG READERS • An imprint of Simon & Schuster Children's Publishing Division • 1230 Avenue of the Americas, New York, New York 10020 • Text copyright © 2017 by Barbara Bottner • Illustrations copyright © 2017 by Michael Emberley • All rights reserved, including the right of reproduction in whole or in part in any form. • ATHENEUM BOOKS FOR YOUNG READERS is a registered trademark of Simon & Schuster, Inc. • Atheneum logo is a trademark of Simon & Schuster, Inc. • For information about special discounts for bulk purchases, please contact Simon & Schuster Special Sales at 1-866-506-1949 or business@simonandschuster.com. • The Simon & Schuster Speakers Bureau can bring authors to your live event. For more information or to book an event, contact the Simon & Schuster Speakers Bureau at 1-866-248-3049 or visit our website at www.simonspeakers.com. • Book design by Ann Bobco • The text for this book was set in Potato Cut. • The illustrations for this book were rendered in pencil and watercolor. • Manufactured in China • 1216 SCP • First Edition • 10 9 8 7 6 5 4 3 2 1 • CIP data for this book is available from the Library of Congress. • ISBN 978-1-4814-5897-9 • ISBN 978-1-4814-5898-6 (eBook)